D1594972

1/21

Wendy's Winter Walk
p, B, M, W Sounds

By Cass Kim, M.A. CCC-SLP
Illustrated by Kawena VK

Wendy's Winter Walk
P, B, M, W Sounds
P.A.C.B. Speech Sounds Series

Cover Design by Kawena VK
Illustrations by: Kawena VK
Illustration Non-Commercial Use Copyright Kawena VK
Illustration Commercial Use Copyright: Cass Kim

FOR ANNABEL AND ELLIOT.
THOUGH WE ARE FAR APART,
YOU ARE ALWAYS IN MY HEART.

My name is Wendy. I love how my name starts with the "Wuh" sound! I purse my lips almost like I'm going to blow a bubble!

Try it!
Wuh Wuh Wendy.

Great work!
Will you come on a walk with me?

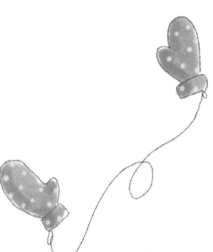

First, my Mom makes sure I'm
wearing my warm clothes:

my mittens,

hat,

and my winter coat.

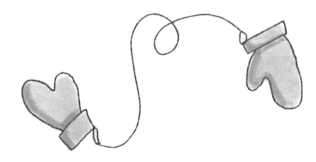

"Bye!" We say to my puppy, Pepper.
Pepper wags his tail and waits in
his warm, blue, bed.

Mom and I slip on our boots and
we're ready to walk.

Next, we wander down the sidewalk.

Mom sees a bunny!
I press my lips together and explode
them in sound.
Bunny. Buh buh bunny.

You try!

I love your great work with talking.

Do you see the bunny?

He has white fur and a bouncy, bubbly
tail, making him blend in with the snow.

Wait!

What's that up in the pine tree?
A blue bird is watching as we walk.
It has a big beak for eating worms.

"Eww, worms for supper?"
I ask my mom.

"Yep. Birds love to eat worms."
Mom smiles as she answers.

Waving goodbye, we walk on.

The wind is whistling.
We practice a whistle too!

Let me hear your whistle — purse
your lips tight and blow soft and slow.

Wow, great work on that whistle!

Brr! The winter weather makes me shiver.

Mom holds my mitten-covered hand in hers as we walk back home.

We see one more animal on our walk.

What can you spy,

waiting in the white snow?

Way back,

behind the purple wagon.

It has brown fur.

A deer!

See his antlers?
We call him a buck.

When we approach my home, I see my snowman waiting patiently.

Mom helps me bundle snow into three balls. One bigger, one medium, one smaller.

We make a baby snowman to stay outside with him.

Can you show me the **biggest** ball?
Where is the medium ball?
What about the smallest ball?

Wonderful pointing work!

When we get inside, Pepper
the puppy is happy to see us.

He wags his tail and begs for pets.

Mom makes us hot cocoa.
How many marshmallows did I get?

Let's count!
One, Two, Three.
Three marshmallows.

What a great walk.
See you next time!

The End

About the Author : Cass Kim

Cass Kim is an established young adult author. She is best known for creating the "Autumn Nights" Charity Anthology Series. In addition to her work as an author, Cass has been a practicing Speech-Language Pathologist with a decade of experience. She holds her Certificate of Clinical Competency from the American-Speech and Hearing Association, as well as a master's degree from Central Michigan University.

About the Illustrator : Kawena VK

Kawena VK grew up in Hawaii with a great fascination for art and nature. She learned through a traditional atelier at the Windward Community College where she was inspired, by her college instructor, to pursue art. She later received her Bachelor of Arts from the University of Hawaii. With her family and friends, Kawena has found a deep sense of happiness through her love for drawing and painting.

Helpful Tips for Parents:

One of the best parts of M, P, B, and W is how visible they are as we say them. A great way to help your child learn these sounds is to pause and ask them to watch you say it. I like to say, "Watch how I say it," and tap my lips to get their attention on my mouth before I say the word.

I only have them practice the sound in isolation (not in the word) twice in this book (like in Wuh Wuh Wendy), because we don't want the pre-word sound practice to become a habit.

Did you know that vision and hearing problems greatly impact speech learning? If your child is struggling to produce sounds, reduced vision or multiple ear infections may be a factor. This is something to bring up to your pediatrician.

For younger children and children with delayed speech sound production, practicing their speech can be very frustrating. Even when they don't get a sound right, positively praising their efforts can help. Throughout the book I demonstrate some ways to praise their efforts, even when they don't hit the target sound perfectly.

This book offers over 200 chances to practice sounds made by the lips (called bilabial sounds).

Another way to keep the practice fun and fresh after you've read this book over and over with your little ones is to have them tell you the story back, using the pictures to guide them.

Want a fun way to practice these lip movements? Blowing bubbles, whistling, and blowing air kisses is a wonderful way to get lips moving in the same range of motion and patterns as needed for these sounds.

These books are not intended to be a substitute for skilled speech therapy treatment. They are meant to be a supplemental addition to practice at home, and a way for families to work together on early sound production activities. If you are concerned about your child's speech, please ask your school system and your pediatrician for a speech therapy evaluation.

For more speech sound activities and information on how reading impacts speech and language development, visit us online:

https://www.pacbspeech.org/home
Check us out on Instagram! @p.a.c.b.speech

CPSIA information can be obtained
at www.ICGtesting.com
Printed in the USA
BVHW021007101120
592960BV00010B/81